MAHOGANY GOES TO WALL STREET

To our nieces & all the girls who look like us,

Embark on your adventures and remember the sky is not the limit! You are #fearlessandintelligent

This is for all the Dreamers, Estamos Juntos. Pura vida !

Imagine it. Plan it. Execute it.

~ Jay & Dev

Mahogany goes to Wall Street
Copyright © 2021 by Janasha Bradford Illustrated by Dev Flowers

Imprint: 12 Eleven Publishing www.mahoganyandfriends.com
Ordering Information: For details, admin@mahoganyandfriends.com

Hardcover ISBN: 979-8-9851325-0-2 Ebook ISBN: ISBN: 979-8-9851325-2-6
Paperback ISBN: 979-8-9851325-1-9
Printed in the United States of America on SFI Certified paper. First Edition

MAHOGANY AND **FRIENDS**
BOOK SERIES

MAHOGANY GOES TO WALL ST

WRITTEN BY:

JANASHA BRADFORD

12ELEVEN
Publishing

ILLUSTRATED BY:

DEV FLOWERS

It was a night like any other night in Charlottesville. Mahogany had finished DINNER, BATHED, and was quietly drawing in her room. She was a girl with a huge imagination and a pretend business.

She had been working all day on her next big invention- a FLYING CANDY MACHINE ! Mahogany loved candy and her favorite uncle who gave her the idea. One day she wanted to own a business just like he did.

It was time for bed. Mahogany's parents knew she would put up a fight.

"Princess, toys away," they said firmly.

Mahogany sighed. "Please, five more minutes! This is my best invention yet and I'm almost done."

Mahogany begged and begged, but her parents did not give in. They cleared her toys, jumped in bed, and snuggled as they read her FAVORITE bedtime story about WALL STREET.

Mahogany's parents knew it was important to fill their child's head with gems for the future. She loved the story and it gave her the IDEA that her Flying Candy Machine could be real! But first, she had to make it to Wall Street because that's where the money was.

Mahogany sat up interrupting the end of her bed time story, "Wait, can we go to Wall Street?" "We can talk about it over breakfast," her father replied. "No fair!" she whined, "I really need to go to get money for my business Mahogany & Friends."

Her parents laughed, "Good night princess! Love you." "Good night! Love you too." she sulked. They kissed her goodnight, tucked her in, and turned out the light. "I'M GOING TO WALL STREET," she whispered.

Mahogany heard snores coming from her parents' room.
She reached for her flashlight and jumped on top of her bed,
"FINALLY, THE PARENTS ARE ASLEEP."

She called out to her three stuffed animal friends in the corner, "Wake up, wake up, guys we're going to Wall Street!"

Mahogany's friends were sleepy, but excited.
"Yayyy, it's a field trip," they cheered.
"SHHHHH! The parents are sleeping. If they wake up we won't be able to go…"
Beary the bear looked puzzled, "What's Wall Street?"

"Wall Street represents the United States financial market," she quoted from her bedtime story, "It is in the financial district of Manhattan, New York."
His eyes sparkled, "NEW YORK CITY?!"

"Yes! New York City!" she smiled. "Wall Street is home to the famous New York Stock Exchange and that's where we're going."
Beary gleamed with excitement.

Ellie the elephant knew Mahogany's adventures often ended in trouble. "Mahogany, are you sure the parents are asleep? Last time we got caught, we couldn't play for an entire week!" Mahogany gave Ellie a side eye, "I'm sure! Stop being a chicken, we're going to Wall Street and the FUN SNATCHERS won't stop us!"

Mahogany took a good look at her business partners, "Wait! We can't go to Wall Street like this. We need to be DRESSED TO IMPRESS! I know just what we need." Mahogany crept out of her room, down the hall, and into the wardrobe that held her parents' work clothes.

She grabbed her dad's big blue blazer, knocking over an empty hanger "CLINK!"
"Oh no!" her eyes grew wide as she heard a fun snatcher on the move.

Mahogany jumped into the wardrobe and closed the door as her parents' bedroom door flew open. Her mother was awake and looking down the dark hallway waiting to hear another sound.

A few seconds went by before the bedroom door closed. She hopped out of the wardrobe and tip-toed back to her room.

"EEEEEK," the floorboard creaked!
"Mahoganyyyy…" her mother called from the bedroom, "is that you?" Mahogany froze in place.

"Yes Mommy it's me, I was getting a glass of milk." Mahogany didn't like to lie, but she couldn't let the fun snatchers stop this adventure!
"Okay, sweetie," her mother replied, "Goodnight! Love you."
"Love you more, Mommy," she ran into her bedroom, shutting the door.

"That was close," said Mahogany as she put on her dad's blazer tossing her friends their clothes.
"Too close," replied an angry Ellie.
"Oh hush!" Mahogany zipped up Ginny's striped dress and helped Ellie slip on Mom's pleated red skirt.

"I look like Daddy," said Beary as he adjusted his polka dot bow tie, "call me Mr. Beary from now on!"
Mahogany laughed and took a good look in the mirror.
"THAT'S MORE LIKE IT, NOW WE'RE READY FOR WALL STREET."

They pulled the blanket over them and watched closely as Mahogany flipped open the pages of her Wall Street book. "Okay, to make this work we have to close our eyes, believe and count to three."
"ONE-TWO-THREE," they all counted together.

WALL ST.

"WHOOSHHH," the Magic of the Imagination happened! They were on Wall Street!
"Come on friends, how about I show you around. Be careful not to bump into any of the sharks and wolves of Wall Street."
Ellie began trembling "Sharks? Wolves?"
Mahogany giggled, "Don't be scared friends! They're just businessmen and women."

Mahogany, Beary, Ellie, and Ginny skipped along Wall Street, they were so happy to be in New York! Mahogany just knew the Flying Candy Machine was going to be a hit! "I. LOVE. IT. HERE!" she said, throwing her head back with joy. "What do you all want to do first?"
"Uh..um..uh.." they stuttered.

Looking at their blank stares, Mahogany realized her friends did not remember anything from the wall street book her parents read her almost every night. "C'mon! Stock market? Monuments? Opening Bell? Do you remember anything?"

STOCK MARKET

STOCKS

Ginny spoke up. "I think… I think..." she mumbled trying to remember something then finally blurted out, "I don't know! What's a stock market?"

Mahogany couldn't believe what she was hearing. "Oh. My. Gosh! All those times my parents read that book! What were y'all doing over there?"

TRADING

SHARE HOLDERS

Mahogany took a deep breath. "Sooo... friends, a STOCK MARKET or stock exchange is like a candy store for grownups where they go to buy pieces of candy called STOCKS. After buying the candy, they are SHAREHOLDERS because they own a small part of the company. They can buy more candy or sell their candy to others; that's called TRADING."
"Really?" interrupted Beary, "I sure do love candy!"

Mahogany knew she could always get her friends attention with candy Now they were listening! "If it's a popular candy that everyone wants, they can make lots of money when selling it. The best candies will get better overtime making them worth more than what was paid for them. Daddy likes to call that CHACHINGCHACHINGBLINGBLING."

CASH

BOND

STOCK

MUTUAL FUND

Investment Portfolio

"Your daddy is soooo silly" said Ginny who couldn't stop laughing.

"But, you have to make sure you have a good mix of candy because Mommy says there is RISK," added Mahogany. "Like, sometimes the price can drop below the amount that was paid for the candy and the buyer will lose money."

The friends came upon the Trinity Church. Beary was in amazement. "Cool!! A castle!" "Nooo, that's not a castle," Mahogany said admiring the structure. "It's the TRINITY CHURCH! Let's play a game."

Ginny knew exactly what game she wanted to play. "Tag, you're it!" she said, tapping her friend's shoulder. They all begin running and playing her favorite game.

They continued on their adventure down Wall Street. They stopped to admire the FEARLESS GIRL STATUE. Mahogany stood next to her striking the same pose. "Hashtag fearless and intelligent" boosted Ellie as she snapped the photo.
"Let's have a race," said Ginny, "ready-set-go!"

They ran down the street to the CHARGING BULL. Mahogany got there first and hopped on the bull like she was in a rodeo. "Ride it cowgirl," they cheered as Mahogany yelled, "Yeehaw!" They were having a blast! Ellie's stomach growled. The friends didn't want to stop playing, but they knew Ellie would become grumpy on an empty tummy.

#FEARLESSANDINTELLIGENT

They all sat down at a juice bar waiting for their avocado toast and OJ. "Let me tell you about our big day at the NEW YORK STOCK EXCHANGE," said Mahogany. "We're going there next!"

HMPH !

"Huh?" said Ginny who was annoyed. "I thought we were going to play tag again."
"Noo, noo, noo." Mahogany replied. "We came to the big city to get big money! Besides, the New York stock exchange is waaaaayyyy better."
"HMPH," an irritated Ginny sighed, "What is that anyway?"

"You see, this is why it's good to pay attention because then you would know that The New York Stock exchange is one of the world's largest stock exchanges. It was created in 1792 and it's also called the BIG BOARD," explained Mahogany, "We were invited to ring the opening bell because our business, Mahogany & Friends, is going public and we're offering an IPO."

"Yayyy! I love ringing bells!" said Beary.

"BOOOOR- ING" grunted Ginny.

"It's not boring! Do you know what an IPO is?" Mahogany asked.

"Nooo!" said the frustrated Giraffe crossing her legs- a sure sign that she was upset. She wanted things to go her way, but was still curious. "Okay, What is this old IPO thing?"

Mahogany wanted Ginny to have a good day. "Ginny, I promise you will love it there! An IPO, which stands for initial public offering, is the first time a company sells its stock to everyone."

Ginny was not interested.

"We're selling our IPO to get extra money, so we can expand and build our Flying Candy Machine!" she said, hoping Ginny would be interested.

"Yes! A Flying Candy Machine!" Ginny started doing her happy dance "Now that sounds like fun!"

They were finishing the last of their breakfast when Mahogany pulled out her Dad's watch from his blazer pocket. It was 8:45am. "Oh no!" she said. "We need to hurry, so we can make it to the New York Stock Exchange on time."

Mahogany hailed a yellow taxi. "Skkrrttt," a taxi quickly stopped. They hopped inside and greeted the driver.

Ellie tapped the taxi driver's shoulder. "CAN YOU PLAY BROWN SKIN GIRL BY BEYONCE?"

The driver agreed and they all started singing their favorite song in unison.

The business partners arrived just in time before the stock market opened at 9:30am. They rushed inside making their way through the busy trading floor.

"Excuse me, Excuse me!" they shouted. The staff greeted them at the podium to ring the OPENING BELL.

Ellie started sweating from stage fright, "S-so many Tvs… and there are so many people here. W-what is an opening bell?"

Mahogany gave Ellie a big hug, "Don't be scared, all your friends are here with you! The opening bell signals the start of the day at the NYSE. It can only be rung by important people like CEO's, celebrities, and us!" Mahogany and Ellie joined Beary and Ginny at the podium as the crowd cheered.

Everyone started buying their IPO stocks right away. "Yayyy! We're going to be able to build our Flying Candy Machine and expand our business. Our IPO is doing great!"

Ginny gave Mahogany a high five "SHOW ME THE MONNEEEYYY!" Mahogany was happy her friends were having a great time on their Wall Street adventure. She drifted off for a few moments taking in the success of their IPO.

Beary was Mahogany's oldest friend; he had been around since she was a baby. "Are you okay?" He always noticed when something was bothering her.

"Yess! I can't believe it." she said, hugging her best friend so tight. "I want to cry. I'm so HAPPY ! ! We put our heads together, planned, and didn't let the fun snatchers stop us!"

Mahogany watched as their IPO price rose. She started doing the happy dance with Ginny and Ellie. Jumping, shaking, moving, and grooving the friends were partying on the trading floor. Mahogany shouted "CHARGE BULL CHARGE."

"What? A Bull? The Charging Bull?!" asked the frightened giraffe. Mahogany laughed. "Nooo it's not a real bull. That's what my dad likes to say when..."

Mahogany was in mid sentence when Ellie interrupted. "Wait, I remember this! Daddy says when prices are going up in the market like a charging bull...It's called a BULL MARKET!"

"Ellie that's right, I'm so proud of you! And the opposite of a Bull Market is a BEAR MARKET when prices go down for a long time."

They all started chanting. "CHARGE, BULL, CHARGE!" the chant grew louder,

"CHARGE, BULL, CHARGE!" and louder,

CHARGE, BULL, CHARGE!

They were having a blast, when all of a sudden...

Mahogany's mother was standing in the doorway with her hands on her hips watching Mahogany jump up and down on the bed. "MAHOGANY!!!" she scolded, "what are you doing with Daddy's blazer, candy, and all of your stuffed animals in your bed?"

Mahogany could tell by the look on her mother's face that she was in big trouble.
"I'm sorry Mommy, but I had to take a trip to Wall Street with my friends," she said in a sweet voice.

Mahogany's mother shook her head and grinned- she thought that was the cutest thing. "Baby, I'm glad that you have a big imagination, but you need to go to sleep. You have school tomorrow. Now, please take off Daddy's blazer and give up those chocolate candies."

She cleared the items from the bed, tucked Mahogany in, and kissed her GOODNIGHT... AGAIN. She placed Mahogany's three stuffed animal friends back in their corner, closed her Wall Street book, and turned out the light.

Mahogany waited for the door to close. She pulled out her handy flashlight. Her friends jumped up and down.

"That was so cool," said Ellie.

"I love Wall Street!" said Ginny.

"The Flying Candy Machine is going to be awesome!" added Beary.

"Charge… {yawn}… bull… {yawn}… charge..." said Mahogany, her eyes began to feel heavy. She lay down on her pillow whispering to her friends "Until next time..." and fell asleep.

THE END.

AUTHOR · JANASHA "JAY" BRADFORD

Janasha Bradford is a financial advisor residing in Charlottesville, Virginia. She is an HBCU Alumni who majored in digital marketing and advertising. She was raised in the inner city of Newark, NJ until her father passed away at the age of eight. Due to a lack of financial literacy, Janasha witnessed her widow mother's challenge of mismanaging a large insurance policy payout that ultimately led to the loss of their family home. This experience made Janasha understand the importance of financial education. She is passionate about filling the void in financial literacy among children, especially in the black and brown communities.

"Thank you so much Mrs.Z! I love you Mommy and The J's. We in this until the wheels fall off KG! " ~Jay

ILLUSRATOR · DEV FLOWERS

Dev Flowers is a self-taught Artist. She is an Afro-latina raised in Limón, Costa Rica. She enjoys making art in different mediums & styles and lives in Fort Hood, Texas with her Army husband & cat.

"Thank you Mamí for seeing me through this process Lo hicimos !"
"I Love you JBF 4lifers !" ~Dev